The Backward Brothers
See the Light
A Tale from Iceland

By Peter Eyvindson
Drawings by Craig Terlson

Northern Lights Books for Children are published by Red Deer College Press
56 Avenue & 32 Street Box 5005 Red Deer Alberta Canada T4N 5H5

Design & Typography by Boldface Technologies Inc.
Printed & Bound in Singapore by Kyodo Printing Co. Pte. Ltd.
The Publishers gratefully acknowledge the financial assistance of
The Alberta Foundation for the Literary Arts, Alberta
Culture & Multiculturalism, the Canada Council,
Red Deer College & Radio 7 CKRD.

Special thanks to Patricia Roy for her assistance
in the preparation of this book.

4 3 2 1

Canadian Cataloguing in Publication Data
Eyvindson, Peter
The backward brothers see the light
Northern lights books for children
ISBN 0-88995-068-7 (bound) ISBN 0-88995-077-6 (pbk.)
I. Terlson, Craig. II. Title. III. Series
PS8559.Y95B3 1991 jc813'.54 C91-091244-0
PZ7.E98Ba 1991

For Kerry, my in-house muse.
– Craig Terlson

For all the gang at summer camp,
especially Andy, Jo, Kathy, Diane, Tim
and maybe even Dennis.
– Peter Eyvindson

PETER EYVINDSON

CRAIG TERLSON

n Iceland, a long time ago, there lived three brothers named Gisli, Erikur and Helgi Bakkabraedur.

They all lived together in an old house, so old that the walls tilted every which way.

Smoke from the fire would never find its way up the chimney, it was so crooked.

These brothers seemed to have only one brain between them for they often acted in a strange and backward manner.

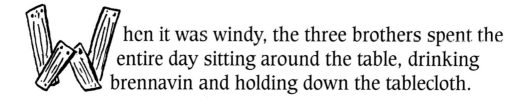

When it was windy, the three brothers spent the entire day sitting around the table, drinking brennavin and holding down the tablecloth.

It was Gisli, one day, who said, "Brothers of mine, I think it is time."

"Time for what?" asked Helgi.

"It is time we built ourselves a new house," said Gisli. "But, brothers of mine, we must make this a very good house. We must have no doors and no windows for they only let in the wind."

ut Gisli," asked Helgi. "Don't we need doors and windows to let out the smoke when we light the fire?"

"That is true," said Erikur. "We must have doors and windows."

"Not if we build a chimney that is straight and true," said Gisli.

"What a wise man you are!" exclaimed Erikur. "Instead of doors and windows, we'll have a chimney that is straight and true."

ut don't we need a door to let us in and out of our new home?" asked Helgi.

"How right you are, Helgi!" said Erikur. "Instead of a chimney, we'll have a door."

And because the brothers did not have much brain between them, so it was decided.

It did not take the Bakkabraedurs long to build their very good house. For even though their brains worked slowly, their bodies gave hard and steady labour.

ne morning, early, Gisli, Erikur and Helgi stood back to look proudly upon their new home with its one narrow door.

"Ah, brothers of mine!" said Gisli. "Our new house is truly a beautiful sight."

"Indeed!" said Erikur. "Doesn't this call for a toast?"

"But where is our brennavin?" asked Helgi.

ecause it was packed away inside their new house, they carefully opened the narrow door and squeezed their way through.

Inside, it was so dark that they stumbled and tripped over each other looking for their brennavin.

When they finally did find the brennavin, the brothers were once more disappointed.

"Brothers of mine," Gisli said. "I cannot see the bottom of my drinking cup."

"Neither can I," said Erikur.

"How will we know if our cups are full or empty?" asked Helgi.

This, indeed, was a great puzzle to the Bakkabraedurs. And it was all the more puzzling to be puzzled in the dark.

"Why, it is so dark in here," said Gisli, "that even my cup is filled with the dark."

"Mine too," said Helgi.

"I – I – I don't believe it," stammered Erikur. "So is mine!"

Turning to show them his cup, Erikur bumped into Helgi who tripped over Gisli who knocked open the door and fell outside.

"Y iya nu yiya!" Gisli exclaimed. "Erikur! Helgi! Come quickly!"

The two brothers stumbled outside.

"Look," Gisli said. "The dark has drained out of my cup and now it is filled with bright morning sunlight."

"So is mine!" said Helgi.

"I can't believe it!" exclaimed Erikur. "The dark has drained out of my cup, too."

The Bakkabraedurs could have spent the entire day admiring their cups, but Gisli got an idea.

"What if we carried our sunlight inside the house?" he asked.

"Gisli, you are so wise!" exclaimed Erikur.

elgi and Erikur watched while Gisli very carefully carried his cup of sunshine to the door.

All morning, the sun had been climbing higher into the sky. At the very same moment as Gisli stepped through the doorway, it just so happened that a single ray of sunlight found its way to the narrow opening.

So, as Gisli poured his cup of sunshine onto the floor, suddenly there it was – a beam of light! Gisli stared in amazement.

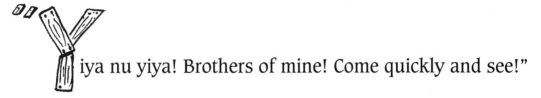"Yiya nu yiya! Brothers of mine! Come quickly and see!"

Carrying their cups, the brothers rushed into the house to see this amazing bit of light. They, too, emptied their cups, and the ray of sunshine began to grow.

Then and there, the Bakkabraedurs knew what they must do. They must bring more of this light into their house.

Taking their cups filled with the dark, they rushed outside, emptied them and filled them with sunshine. Back and forth they rushed, taking out the dark and carrying back in the sparkling sunshine.

All morning long, the mad rush continued. And as the sun grew higher, more light poured through the door.

"Ah, how wise we are, my brothers," Gisli said. "See how our home is getting brighter!"

*T*hen, as the sun began to settle in the west, Gisli made another important discovery.

"Look!" panted Gisli. "We've taken so many cups of dark from our house that all outside is growing dark."

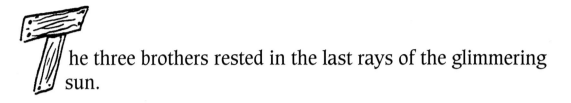

he three brothers rested in the last rays of the glimmering sun.

"Hurrah!" they exclaimed as they watched the sun disappear.

"This calls for a toast," said Erikur.

"But where is our brennavin?" asked Helgi.

he Bakkabraedurs rushed through the narrow door. But they were sadly disappointed. The house inside was as dark as all outside.

"Why, I cannot see the bottom of my drinking cup," said Helgi.

"Neither can I," said Erikur.

"Brothers of mine!" said Gisli. "Do not be discouraged. This dark inside our house is a nuisance. If we are ever to succeed in clearing it from our house, we must begin very early in the morning. Let us go to bed now so we will be well rested and ready to work very hard first thing in the morning."

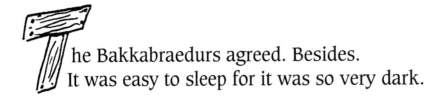

The Bakkabraedurs agreed. Besides.
It was easy to sleep for it was so very dark.

PETER EYVINDSON

For Peter Eyvindson, writing and storytelling go hand in hand. After completing Bachelor degrees in Arts and Education, he became a teacher-librarian, partially fulfilling his passion for books and teaching children about them. In 1983, he decided to indulge his passion full time and has since then written six very popular children's books, all of them bestsellers. Peter Eyvindson lives in Clavet, Saskatchewan.

CRAIG TERLSON

Craig Terlson's versatility is the source of a career ranging from award-winning newspaper graphics to children's book illustration. After completing his Fine Arts degree at the Alberta College of Art, he began illustrating for an extensive list of book, magazine and advertising clients across North America. He is currently at work on a science series for children. Craig Terlson lives in Winnipeg, Manitoba.